T0065256

A COSMIC AWAKENING OF RELATIONSHIPS BEYOND US

A COSMIC
AWAKENING OF
RELATIONSHIPS
BEYOND US

CARLA BOATNER

A COSMIC AWAKENING OF RELATIONSHIPS BEYOND US

iUniverse books may be ordered through booksellers or by contacting:

iUniverse
1663 Liberty Drive
Bloomington, IN 47403
www.iuniverse.com
844-349-9409

ISBN: 978-1-6632-1714-1 (sc)
ISBN: 978-1-6632-1715-8 (e)

Library of Congress Control Number: 2021901113

Print information available on the last page.

iUniverse rev. date: 07/23/2021

This book is dedicated to the life lessons of love witnessed from grandparents, parents, brothers and sisters, friends, my daughter Summer Rose Crawford and all the collective consciousness offered while writing this book, which is, indubitably, beyond us.

CONTENTS

PREFACE

This book gives the reader a conscious awakening through serendipitous experiences. The characters in the book discover their interconnected relationship with the development of the cosmos as they develop their inner strength. The love fortified within each character out of chaos is splendid for the reader to cognitively digest and absorb the nutrients of love. The reader will discover the magical synchronicities of love's healing powers. The book gives an individualized secret road map for how to renew and restore relationships through love for optimal growth.

INTRODUCTION

The Beyond Us is a place where any relationship can go. All you need to travel to the Beyond Us is a vehicle of enlightenment. You will know a couple who are in the Beyond Us, because they will have the capacity to be who they are authentically and give each other the space to be genuinely themselves. Few couples make it to the Beyond Us, but when couples do arrive to the Beyond Us, the results are harmonious, and true freedom is exemplified. These are stories of couples who, through love, learned the path of least resistance and, as a result, accomplished the Beyond Us. The journey to the Beyond Us might be hard or easy, but it is necessary for relationships to thrive.

CHAPTER 1

THE FIRST HAPPENSTANCE

On their auspicious sixtieth vow-renewal celebration, Joe and Liz unveiled their love story and their raw, uncut journey to the Beyond Us. During Liz and Joe's vow renewal on the planet Third Eye on June 16, 2060, Liz said, "Let's be one hundred percent honest. Our love story is more like a twisted love story. Nonetheless, it is our love story to the Beyond Us. It all started on January 1, 2060, years prior."

On that night, Liz decided to travel to planet Root. She could not wait; she knew deep inside that night would be great. She felt in the very fiber of her being that she would meet the potential One. Liz made a vow that she would marry whomever she coupled with next, and she believed this last coupling partner was, luckily, coming soon. She had been reared to believe a person was undignified if he or she had sex before a full circling partnership was established. Liz had been with a number of men. She dared not tell a soul, so she did not tell anyone. Liz could not even admit the number of men she'd slept with to herself, for Liz had to be perfect, even if that meant lying to herself and deceiving others about her indiscretions.

With being perfect in mind, Liz picked out her clothing for that night: an orange bodysuit that fit her body like a glove and matching orange heels high enough to reach the heavens but comfortable enough to dance the hell out of. Liz could groove and move like no other woman could; when she danced, it was as if she were dancing with every fiber in her aura radiating. Her hair was orange with red highlights, naturally standing out. Liz was perfectly orange; even her nails were orange, and they were shaped flawlessly. Liz was determined to be perfect that night and match from her head to her toes. She took hours curling her hair, and then, right before leaving her home, she rinsed her hair out for a more natural look. Because of all the heat and hair spray, Liz's hair stuck straight up on the top of her head. She looked as if she had been electrically shocked.

After her initial attempt to shampoo her curls did not work, Liz had to shampoo her hair several times to get her hair back to its natural state. Once Liz achieved her natural textured wave, she was sure to have a great time, she thought. She looked at herself in the mirror, applied last touches of makeup and lipstick, and then said, "Perfect!"

She walked out the door with confidence, got in her space car, and levitated straight to planet Root. Root was the best club and farthest planet from her gossiping family and judgmental associates. Liz was private, especially with family and friends. She had to be mysterious, or else she would be ridiculed. Liz often felt something was missing in her life. She felt forced to be something that didn't feel normal to her natural state. Liz had to be perfect, so she portrayed perfection, even at the expense of unauthenticity. Liz did whatever she was asked to do, and she did it well.

In reality, what was missing in Liz's life was not a man—Liz was missing herself. Liz did not have a complete identity of her own. Heading to the Beyond Us was not always the quest for Liz, but love had a way of helping couples find enlightenment. Only over time did Liz mature and learn to recognize her own voice.

Liz loved to party. She had a freaky side. Liz hardly knew who she was, for she kept a part of herself a secret from herself and from family and friends. Liz desired an authentic life but did not understand how to obtain such a lofty goal. She said to herself often,

"What would they think?" or "How fast would they disown me if my family and friends knew my imperfections?" So off to the farthest planet she went for some good ole fun times.

Once she arrived at planet Root, her barcode was scanned on her wrist, for energetic currency was required for an entrance fee. Liz was cleared to come into planet Root. She said in amazement, "Wow, planet Root's ambience is out of this galaxy. It has me feeling nostalgic!"

The doorkeeper said, "Please leave your shoes here, for shoes carry energies from your past, and these floors were made to create new memories and require bare feet."

The floors also had been created to self-heat and felt warm on Liz's bare feet. Liz thought, *My orange heels were going to get the hell danced out of them anyway, and besides, this hot foam material is perfect to keep me comfortable with no shoes on anyway.* She thought to herself, *This place is astonishing*, and her thought projected onto a large screen on the wall of the main dance floor, where Liz would be dancing any minute. All positive thoughts projected onto the club's large screen; this kept the club's positive energy waves soaring. The walls helped to keep the morale up as well, with kinetic energy keeping all the upbeat vibes in motion. The dark-space-matter cleanser made of black tourmaline and the black tourmaline vacuum machine were responsible for trapping negative energy in the club and taking it out of the atmosphere.

Liz was in awe. She thought, *This place is so it right now. These rustic earth-tone colors are an aphrodisiac. I know anything is possible tonight.* Liz felt it deep within her heart.

Little did Liz know she was correct; that night, she would meet her forever. That was how Joe and Liz met, there on planet Root. The vibes were electric. Liz and Joe could feel the music's vibrations in each other's bones pulling them closer to each other. The music's vibrations in their bones boomed in their hearts, in their souls, and right to each other's forever. They were both perfectly riding the rhythmic waves with the DJ's sacral, deep house red music playing loudly. With each beat, they felt free to be open, centered, and connected.

Liz felt her hands getting hotter. She knew something magical was taking place.

Joe interjected, saying, "It is the red sacral drinks activating our red sacral chakras." Joe, like Liz, felt on top of the planet.

Joe and Liz literally floated on top of planet Root's atmosphere and bumped into each other.

On the occasion of their vow renewal, Joe looked at Liz said, "I remember so clearly your kissed-by-twenty-four-karat-gold skin and your diamond-like, bright, sparkling hazel eyes. Your bodysuit was a spicy hot orange, and your hair was so free, with big, long waves crashing into each other. Your on-fire orange aura kept me intrigued. It nearly set me on fire, literally and figuratively."

Liz said, "As I remember it, you almost got burned by my energetic flames coming out of my hands. The music radiating through my body transferred successfully and activated my superpowers ablaze."

Joe said, "I guess the red sacral music and red sacral drinks were strong." Joe and Liz laughed while holding each other tightly. Joe went on to say, "From the start, it was your flames that captivated my heart."

Liz said, "After sixty years of journeying with you, Joe, to the Beyond Us, I still heat up as you poetically sing my praises!" It was not always Joe's strong point to communicate his admiration of Liz or to recognize her verbally in a positive manner and sing of her glorious beauty.

Liz grabbed Joe's hand and looked him in his eyes, recalling his gorgeous olive skin, golden-honey eyes, burnt-orange carrot hair, and orange bodysuit to die for. She was drooling just thinking about his chiseled body in that suit sixty years ago. Liz had played it cool, but her flames could not contain themselves at first sight, and she'd lit up.

Joe said, "Liz, let's not get too carried away." They both laughed. It was not a typical laugh but a harmonious sound of joyful pleasure.

"Yes, the good old days." Liz recalled it all too well. "It was the day we decided to go full circle and began journeying to the Beyond Us."

At first sight, Joe had floated right into Liz's orange flames.

Liz, as if in a trance, had thought, *With this coupling, I can atone for my shortcomings in all other relationships, sacrificing myself for our full circling, for my higher self will be in charge.*

Joe shook Liz back into the room as he gazed into her eyes, just as he had done that night more than sixty years ago when he'd floated into her life and she'd captivated him with her orange flames. Liz grabbed Joe's hand as he floated with her. Immediately, she felt amazement, as the stars on Third Eye were shining brightly. Liz felt one with the universe, and Joe felt one with the universe too.

***

Coupling balanced Joe and Liz well by showing them their own nonuseful patterns, and that night was the start of awakening. Liz let her facade down—not by choice, as it was not allowed at Club Root—and Joe left his dark side out the door as well. That meant no pretense, and they coupled over and over in a way that neither of them ever had before. Joe never knew Liz would allow herself to rain within his cloud of glory, but with Liz, this happened after much coupling. They both cried tears of joy because Joe learned to give of himself to please others, and to receive pleasure in that moment, they became one; a complete circle formed.

That night, as Joe floated with Liz in his arms, he flew with shooting-star speed as Liz's bright orange flaming hands lit up the sky from galaxy to galaxy, and the coupling happened repeatedly—for sixty years to come. Liz and Joe thought, *Oh, praise the coupling for balancing us so we could move to the Beyond Us and operate in our purpose, which is for all the greater good of existence.*

In honor of their coupling, Liz and Joe made a vow to each other for life. Liz and Joe stated, "We will always look beyond us for the greater good and peaceable oneness with the universe."

Coupling taught Liz and Joe to open their third-eye chakras. To have access to the Beyond Us took hard work, as both had blocks they had to overcome outside of Club Root's positive atmosphere. After overcoming their individual insecurities, they became a shooting star. Joe floated in the beginning but learned to rocket with Liz's flaming hands across the dark void of atmosphere like a shooting star.

CHAPTER 2

◆

NUCLEAR FUSION OF THE RELATIONSHIP

Joe and Liz, day after day, fought about everything, little, big, and in between. The dark matter was in control, and they were stuck in a vacuum full of "I am right, you should know why I am right, you are wrong, and you should know why you are wrong." Liz and Joe's joining together to create something bigger initially looked like pure chaos: bigger arguments, bigger yelling matches, bigger issues, and bigger concerns, depending on Liz's and Joe's differing perspectives on the matter. As they came from two different family backgrounds, that type of fighting was to be expected. Each partner thought his or her way was the right way, with no clue they could create what was right and what was wrong, tailored to their individualized relationship as a couple. Liz's and Joe's family-inherited rules of right and wrong overshadowed their own relationship insights.

Liz had been reared on a planet of dignitaries and had a right and wrong reason for everything she did. She had a right and wrong way of being for everything that related to life, and she imposed those beliefs on Joe. She imposed those beliefs on all who came across her aura field. People did not listen to Liz, but usually when people were caught in proximity, Liz would impose her values regardless of their willingness to hear her right or wrong judgmental commentary.

Liz thought her house had to be perfect and would fight with Joe if it was not cleaned to perfection daily. Liz thought, *When I go out this door, every hair on my head and every hair on Joe's head had better be in place.* Liz and Joe never got to experience the now. She watched everything she did, for fear of the dignitaries disowning her or the social elites criticizing her. Liz was in denial of the fact that the dignitaries had already disowned her when they found out she used her free time to party on planet Root. Dignitaries did not party; they sat at a round table with hot cups of tea, watching others party and laughing at how despicable those so-called barbarians looked at the party. Liz felt she was right and justified—it was her way or the highway. Little did she know she was also considered a barbarian by her own people for settling for someone from a planet where everything went.

Throughout the marriage, Liz had various lists: a list for chores, a list for top money-making jobs, and a list for how to breathe. These lists were all for Joe to fit in with the dignitaries. Liz had a noble father; he worked hard to provide for his family, he gave his wife his increase, he was pleasing to his wife, and he was pleasing to Liz. Liz was the only child. She learned early on that love meant gifts and approval from other dignitaries.

Joe felt not good enough for Liz, her family, and her friends. Every list given confirmed his self-proclaimed not-good-enough status. Joe, after meeting Liz's family a few times, including at the wedding ceremony, decided he would not go around her family, and if he ran into her family, the interaction lasted no longer than a few minutes at a time. Joe spoke carelessly every other word and enjoyed conversing loosely. It was a struggle for him to watch his mouth and demeaner, and he felt fake when he had to do so, so he kept his distance. That meant Liz went to functions alone.

Liz's bodysuit no longer fit; she was eating to compensate for companionship. Joe could feel his manhood shifting, and that demasculinizing energy wanted to explore other women—women who might boost Joe's aura field and not fuss or complain. Joe had been reared on a do-as-you-please planet with no guidance but the beat of his own drum. Joe's mother and father were both self-seeking. Joe had been reared to be self-seeking; he would not have eaten or known how to survive otherwise. Joe's parents had left him to fend for himself for months at a time since age nine. Joe bathed whenever he could smell himself, which was a few days after the rest of the world could smell his garbage-scented odor. His underarms smelled like onions, and his crevasse smelled like rotten meat. Joe's hair was dirty too, and his teeth had a yellow film.

Sixty years before, Joe had showered, brushed his teeth, and put on cologne. Little had Liz known when she met him at Club Root in his superb state that Joe had not been taught to clean up after himself, had not learned hygiene routines, and played space games and women games to the extreme. Truly, opposites had attracted that night! Liz had not been in her natural state either; she never went clubbing, danced with no shoes on, or styled her hair for a natural look. The two were total opposites and in for the transformation of a lifetime.

As soon as Liz left, Joe ripped up her various lists, figuratively and literally. He left the pieces of her lists in each woman he coupled with. Of course, Liz had no knowledge of the women Joe coupled with. Joe knew how to displace his anger; he would displace his anger by playing space games or by playing women games. Joe was no innocent man, and he was not finished making Liz pay for not accepting him as a space game player, not doing as Joe said, and not pleasing Joe at all costs. Joe came full circle with Liz because he felt he was doing her a favor; he knew her family were dignitaries, and he did not want to bring shame on Liz for coupling with a barbarian.

Liz began to find the pieces of her lists throughout the atmosphere, as gravity was not in charge; in space, her lists floated right on by. In that space, Liz knew there was something wrong with her and Joe's relationship. Liz could not pick up all the pieces of the relationship. Every time she tried to pick up the pieces of her lists given to Joe, she would bounce backward. Liz bounced backward due to her focus on his mistakes, which was not helping in building a healthy relationship with Joe, herself, or anyone else.

Soon enough, Liz understood that her destructive barbarian thinking was part of the problem. She tried to pick up the pieces, but the pieces were everywhere. Joe was so used to mess that he did not notice his life was messy. Liz felt overwhelmed by his drama. She felt unheard, and she felt useless in all her attempts to turn Joe into the man her father was. Her attempts were inoperable, as Joe became more combative. Liz and Joe were feeling dysfunctional in the story they told themselves.

Liz wanted Joe to be successful according to her timeline and on her terms. Liz tried to teach him how to drive levitating space cars. Driving space cars from her planet home of the dignitaries required much concentration—concentration Joe did not require on his planet, where everything went. Liz tried to help Joe find a career. Joe felt hopeless that Liz would not allow him room to mature on his own and in his own season.

Initially, Joe did not mind the story, even with its deceit, if Liz was in his story, and Joe was still able to be in other women's stories to stroke his ego and feel good after Liz heaped disappointment upon him. Joe had learned since a child to fend for himself, and his mother and father were also not there for him emotionally. They did not answer questions honestly, never took responsibility for Joe or their actions, and left Joe day in and day out to figure out life for himself. From Joe's upbringing, he was defensive, resourceful, and self-motivated and had a high level of resiliency. Every time Liz tried to help Joe, he felt demeaned, inferior, violated, and sheepish. Joe's parents did not give him positive attention, and he felt like oil in water with others, unable to mix, take responsibility for his actions, and see room for improvement to thrust forward.

Liz was a servant; she had been taught to serve her family and serve her friends. She felt worth from helping others, and that was one thing Joe refused to let Liz do. Joe's scars were deep from years of emotional cuts, hidden within his heart like cartilage built up on deep cuts. Therefore, when Liz complained or gave unsolicited suggestions, Joe would break away and cheat, for the pain was agonizing. Liz was massaging thick cartilage, and for Joe, it felt unbearable. Joe, although not liking the massage of his emotions, required the breaking down of emotional cartilage for full capacity of his heart to be used. Joe used other women to soothe his hurt ego and calm his feelings of being let down by pleasing each woman and meeting his need for acceptance.

Liz felt uncomfortable when visiting Joe's home planet, where the rules for family were nonexistent. No one in Joe's family was full-circled; he was the first one in his family to get full-circled. Further, conversations were vulgar and unseemly on the planet where Joe had grown up. Liz felt liberated and, at the same time, unnerved by Joe's culture.

Every time Joe came close to Liz's heart, she would yell at him and bring up the pieces of her fragmented and torn-apart lists. The story she told herself was that Joe tore apart the lists with every woman he slept with, and every list he ripped to shreds. Liz could not see that her lists were part of the pieces breaking the peace of their love story. Joe was so angry and frustrated with Liz's to-do list and not-to-do list that he began telling his story of resentment and regret of their coupling. As Liz and Joe told their stories, the pieces became more and more fragmented, until they were so irritated with each other that they stopped fighting and spun out with fast momentum in opposite directions.

Liz and Joe did not realize, for the lack of proof, that a seed of love took root. Liz and Joe's relationship seemed dead, but it was alive! Joe and Liz did not see the roots attached and alive, for they saw only the dead parts of their relationship, but something remarkable was taking place. Liz stopped fighting with Joe over his cheating, and Joe stopped fighting with Liz over her to-do and not-to-do lists. Joe was tired of himself but had no idea how to change. Liz was tired of herself, the rigidity, doing as the dignitaries approved but not being true to herself, and risking regrets. Liz and Joe's relationship was assailing and draining. Joe was floating by, and Liz was burning her way through existence.

While in the fighting ring, on multiple occasions, before and after the spun-out state, Joe and Liz felt excited about the venting of each other's anger and rage. Through the story they told each other, they repeatedly stayed in self-created chaos. Joe knew in his heart if he ever stopped fighting with Liz, he would fall back in love with

Liz. Deep down, Joe understood the truth: he was still in love with Liz, but he knew she was not going to accept the cheating, lying, or defensive behaviors. Joe was clear that Liz no longer would accept his infidelities, but he was not confident in himself to change.

Joe resented Liz's ability to hold him accountable for his indiscretions, so he decided to date Ivy, a woman he'd cheated on Liz with prior to the spun-out condition. Joe thought, *Ivy does all the things Liz will not do*, so he started seeking revenge with Ivy. He learned to drive dignitary cars with Ivy, he learned to be faithful to Ivy, and he learned to put a woman first—not that Ivy required to be put first, but Joe wanted to prove he could love a woman and, in the process of loving that woman, also make Liz resent the spun-out state and be jealous. Joe plotted to see if Liz would be jealous; then he would know he was the winner of the fight.

Liz knew Joe was dating Ivy and honored the dignitary women's code, which said, "When you know a man is in a relationship with someone, you do not partake in coupling." Joe also started saving money for a home on planet Root, where he and Liz had met, as he felt that would really fire Liz up and make her regret the spun-out reality. Liz was mad. Why could Joe not do all that growth in a relationship with her? Yet Liz was happy for Joe. She did not care who inspired him to be better; it positively impacted his lifestyle regardless and, indirectly, would be better for their future. Liz was loving and loved Joe, but she did not know how to love Joe as Joe needed to be loved without causing herself pain and suffering with Joe's escapades. Joe cheated and was not emotionally available for Liz or even for himself. He was lost in Liz's eyes, and she was not found in his heart.

However, over time, people could discover love by growing into their own state of authenticity. Liz took a hard look in the mirror, and she did not recognize herself a hundred extra pounds later. She struggled with her new weight. Liz had been her best weight when she met Joe, and over the years, with all the fighting, cheating, and needing to be validated, she had overeaten fattening foods. Like Joe, she cheated, but her cheating was on herself and the body she wanted. Liz wanted to respect herself, but with her cheating on her health and the health of the relationship, she lacked self-respect. Liz understood that it was time to stop focusing on Joe and on the dignitaries and start seeking to love herself unconditionally, for better or for worse. Liz started eating healthier, working out, working on being authentic by focusing on what made her feel good daily, and working on increasing a positive outlook on life.

Liz saw Joe as a manipulator and a self-seeking, arrogant prick, but Liz played a role too. She was too selfless and appeased others to her own detriment. Joe saw Liz as a know-it-all control freak but with no self-control to stop appeasing the dignitaries or overeating. Both of them kept their stories of "It is everyone else's fault and not my own fault" going until they both met Sophia. They were spun out but living together, for both had nowhere else to go until they saved up money. They were spun out in the mental and emotional aspects of the intricate relationship. Liz was like an outlaw, and Joe was too clean to go back home; his aura was too upbeat for his old planet. They still did not know how to coexist with each other. Joe continued to date Ivy, and Liz started dating herself. The two individuals lived in the same home but miles apart.

CHAPTER 3

SPUN OUT

Living together but spun out meant Liz and Joe had failed each other. They had failed at knowing how to love each other. Neither was tuned in to or turned on to the station of respect and what that looked like for them individually. Liz and Joe thought love was control, and if they could not control each other or, in Joe's case, lacked control, there was nothing left in the relationship.

Little did they know that the death of the false perceptions they clung to so dearly needed to happen for an authentic relationship to emerge. They did not comprehend that control was an illusion. Joe had no rules and, therefore, no issues, he thought. Liz had rules and thought her rules gave her control. Liz and Joe presumed love was control or out of control, and neither of them was right. Love was the space that Liz and Joe had to learn to offer each other to respect their total selves. Liz, still living with Joe, never told a dignitary about their spun-out state.

Liz was humiliated about the relationship not working out—so much so that she denied the spun-out state with all who would have judged and ridiculed her. Liz could not be vulnerable and bare her soul with her family or peers, so she maintained a facade.

Joe flaunted his spun-out state by blaming it all on Liz, never considering his cheating as part of the breakdown in their relationship. Joe was so accustomed to lying to himself and others that he did not notice his lies were now discovered. Joe maintained several women at one time; he enjoyed juggling them for different reasons, mostly so they could stroke his ego when he was having a hard time with Liz or one of his other various women. On rare occasions, in front of visiting friends and family, Joe would scream at the top of his lungs to embarrass Liz. He would scream, "I am no longer your man!"

Liz would say, "Meet my man," pointing to Joe.

He would again scream at the top of his lungs, "I am not your man!" In a demeaning fashion, he would say, "You spun this relationship out." He was like a child who blamed everything on the kid down the street, such as his falling off his bike, when he knew ahead of time his bike's tires were flat in the first place.

Joe continued being Mr. Everything Goes, and Liz continued being Liz Know-It-All. They lived together, still fighting for love in all the wrong ways. Liz, the perfect one, went out on the town. She thought, *I am spun out. It is time to wet my hair as I did when I met Joe and go find someone interesting. I just want to have fun.* Little did she know the fun was happening with Joe and his mistress Ivy. Liz could not bring herself to date anyone else, so she continued working on her self-love and confidence.

Ivy was Joe's off-and-on girlfriend since he was with Liz. Ivy watched on the sidelines of their relationship and hated Joe for stringing her along. Ivy regretted what she did to tear down a fellow woman's home, or so she thought, for she really did not have the authority to tear down Joe and Liz's home; only they did. Ivy had just become part of the female planet power movement on planet V. V stood for *Vagina*. Ironically, planet V was not about vaginas but about women having purpose beyond having a vagina, for women were more than a female mucus membrane. One of the rules on V was to make amends with women one had violated purposefully or by accident.

Ivy had, on multiple occasions, slept with Joe without inquiring if he was married. Joe was so unpolished that no one knew he was taken. He was useless otherwise, but women knew he was okay in bed, and it was better than horrible sex to have okay sex with selfish

Joe. Joe was selfish in bed but good at what he found pleasurable. Joe was like his parents; his father fought for nothing and kept a new girlfriend monthly as a result. His mother was selfish, partied hard, and shopped through life, taking no responsibility for whomever she tore down to get what she wanted. Anyone who crossed her paid with rumors and their things being stolen, and Joe was following suit of both his parents.

The Beyond Us agent Sophia became Joe and Liz's mediator for lovers lost in the story they told themselves. Ivy paid for this service to be sent to their home, as she felt bad about her part. Ivy was naive; she asked no questions while sleeping with Joe, assuming he was single. She never had imagined a full-circle man would be like Joe, and for that assumption, she suffered. When she found out Joe was full-circled, she was already accustomed to the coupling and stayed.

Ivy knew Joe still loved Liz, because sometimes while they were coupling, she would hear him stop himself from uttering Liz's name. Ivy one day packed up all her things and left. Before she left, she left a note:

> Dear Joe,
>
> You deceive women. You did not tell me when we met that you were still coupled with Liz. I know you still love Liz, but your pride is in the way, so I am leaving. I am never coming back, and I will not be part of the love triangle anymore. I cannot respect myself anymore while staying with a cheating man, and you are against womanhood's survival.
>
> Sincerely,
> Ivy

Joe, in shock, read the letter over and over again. He never really read Liz's to-do and not-to-do lists, so this was a wake-up call for him.

Joe was finally by himself; Liz had left him, and now his mistress had left him. He thought to himself, *Oh, what will I do?* Then Joe snapped out of it. He remembered his little black book with the other women he had on hold for such a time, which those two naive women knew nothing about. Joe went to his list of women, looking for one who would be his next conquest, and his heart melted. Something inside him paused in the process. He felt a change. He felt that Liz and Ivy, for the first time, were trying to get him to see himself.

That night, instead of contacting a woman, he talked to Liz. Joe told Liz everything. He told her about the other women, and he told her he was scared of losing the only woman he really loved: Liz.

Years prior, Liz would have gone crazy at the conversation, but that day, she felt compelled to listen, and she did listen to Joe compassionately. In that conversation, Liz could hear Joe's pattern unfold: his cheating had nothing to do with her being not good enough; rather, it was about his lack of self-love. He was accustomed to blaming others for his need for instant gratification.

Liz spoke from her heart. She told Joe how she was required to chase perfection and never felt good enough. She felt not good enough with her family and friends and wanted to please everyone to fit in but was failing at pleasing everyone. Ironically, it was a good failure, because she was discovering who she was, not who she was made to pretend to be, and she was good enough.

Joe told Liz, "I love you. I knew our full circle was over. Thanks for giving us space to have a fresh start."

Liz said, "Joe, maybe we did not need a fresh start; maybe we needed to have this moment. We dignitaries do not know how to be vulnerable." Looking up while glued to Joe's golden eyes, she said, "Hmm," laughing under her breath. "Both of us just did it! We became empathetic and compassionate towards each other. This is the holy place couples go to!"

In that hour, Joe and Liz unveiled, coupled repeatedly, and reunited authentically in their full circle. Joe ran some hot bathwater for Liz and put red rose oil, red rose petals, and little red sacral bath soap beads in the water. He took her shoes off, unzipped her orange bodysuit, took her red panties off, and took her red bra off; laid her down on the plush red velvet bed; and massaged her body with warm red sacral body oil. Joe made fists and rubbed his knuckles into Liz's back. He then used the tips of his fingers, massaging them like tumbleweeds rubbing up and down on the pavement of her body. Liz felt relaxed and pampered.

After her massage, he led her to be submerged in love. When she stepped into her hot bath, Liz soaked and smelled the rose oil soap Joe handpicked to saturate her body. Liz felt Joe's love directed immensely for her for the first time deeply. Liz could feel Joe unselfishly rubbing her back to bring her to ecstasy in the bathtub without a thought about himself. Joe prepared a large basin of hot water, took his clothing off, and got into the bathtub with Liz. He poured water onto Liz's hair and began shampooing her scalp vigorously with rose-oil-based soap, which could be used to clean Liz's entire body, and he used the basin full of hot water to wash the soap out of Liz's hair. Then Joe turned Liz toward him and said, "Liz, I washed you from head to toe. This symbolizes how I will love you, all of you, for the rest of our lives." He held Liz in the bathtub heart to heart, head to head, fully connected.

Now Liz and Joe's key was locked eternally, and in that moment, their earth love child, Rick, was planted in Liz's womb and ready to grow.

CHAPTER 4

RECONNECTED

Joe and Liz, after years of combat, had energy that could transmute their ordinary love into something great and meaningful in the form of Rick. Sophia politely showed up at Joe and Liz's door and knocked. Sophia had knocked on the door on several occasions; however, Joe and Liz usually were too busy being right to hear the knocking. Sometimes the knocking was heard when Joe saw Liz helping others see their way with her energetic orange flames naturally shining. Sometimes the knocking was heard when Joe was coupling with Liz and forgetting about himself while pleasing Liz. While Joe was in the moment of surrender, a circle would form as he floated by, and Liz's hands glowed brightly with orange heat radiating. Each time Sophia knocked on Joe and Liz's door, they trained their ears for the sound of the Beyond Us. The Beyond Us had a sound of om. The Beyond Us could be heard only in the stillness and knowing of the collective peace. Perhaps it was the pieces of all stillness coming together.

Sophia was relentless in her knocking. Joe and Liz got closer to the door so they could hear the stillness within each other. With each step Joe and Liz took closer to the door, they became less identified with being right and telling their stories, and they began allowing the story that complemented them to emerge. Any couple could access the Beyond Us; they just needed compassion and empathy for the sake of loving each other with their actions.

Joe and Liz rubbed and rubbed; it was sensual at times, it was anger turned at themselves at times, and sometimes it involved plain ole annoying tendencies. However, the heat kept getting hotter and hotter, until Liz and Joe burned up all reactivity, anger, resentment, irritation, and wasted energy and transformed their minds by transmitting enlightenment within each other's highest self.

Joe and Liz had been fighting and fighting with nothing to show for it, but after having what did not work right in front of them, they began to do the opposite of what did not work. Joe stopped cheating and ripping up Liz's lists, Liz stopped making to-do and not-to-do lists, and they decided to give each other space to grow and figure out how they complemented each other. There was so much musical energy built up and pulling in toward each other that when Joe and Liz transmuted their energy for the greater good of each other, it produced the sun. While they were coupling, Liz's hands heated up and burst into pure light, radiating heat enough to warm up planet Earth, and Joe's body rotated in that moment. Together they created the sun that was responsible for Earth's light and heat and that gave light to their son, Rick, the representative for planet Earth.

Liz was exhausted with feeding and taking care of Rick. Joe and Liz began breaking down, and she was able to admit she did not know everything. Joe was able to admit that having no rules did not always mean freedom. For the first time, Joe made a joke about the old lists Liz had created and said they might have been useful now, since Liz's pregnancy brain was active, and she was starting to forget things. As the sun rotated, one could see the sunspots on the couple's surface; they were wise. Liz and Joe reared their son, the representative for Earth, with love, truthfulness, and wisdom learned from their errors.

Sophia knocked, and as a result of their listening, Liz's and Joe's third-eye chakras lit up and became activated. Sophia knocked on the doors of all who dared to listen, and Joe and Liz told a story of allowing that deep knowing to take over. There were many Beyond Us agents. Sophia was the agent who knocked on one's door and said, "Enough *me*. Get still. Be still. You are, in fact, the stillness that is unquestionably the Beyond Us. When we speak of Beyond Us, we are speaking of the personalization of things, ownership. We defend things, defend ourselves, defend our past, defend our thought processes, and defend our position out of a place of 'I am not good enough.' We are not aware of the all in all and how the connections Beyond Us are not lacking or needing anything. It just is. It is the all that there is—om—and will ever be, the space to be. The Beyond Us!"

CHAPTER 5

••◆••

THE EARTH

Rick was conceived by Liz the know-it-all and Joe, Mr. Everything Goes, working together in harmony. Their vibration was that of ultimate joy. Through joyful vibrations twenty-three years and six months prior to their sixtieth vow renewal, Rick, their Earth, was born. Rick was not born by chance. Rick was a demonstration of balance, the same balance required to keep Earth ever evolving and safe. Sophia felt the Beyond Us was up to something altruistic, but it was time for her to be transferred, so for the first time, Liz and Joe were officially ready to be home with wisdom fully embraced. That wisdom was always with them now, fully activated. Earth was no longer just a rock, which Rick could not take credit for, since his parents had collided into each other. Liz's glowing orange hands and Joe's floating had created something special called Earth. Liz and Joe gave their son, Rick, the distance to grow, and in that space, the love was endless.

Rick, reigning and ruling over Earth, required an intense focus on organization to accomplish his mission. Rick had to master himself. Knowing about his parents' history and understanding the obstacles they'd had to overcome taught Rick to keep his balance. Rick was careful to watch his checks and balances and keep in check his know-it-all ego and the everything-goes aspects of himself from his parents. Day after day, he devoted his life to balance. It was perfect, but the

Beyond Us was not complete with his transformation. His perfections were recognized and even admired. He took his mother's and father's energy and created synchronicity. Rick had the ability to compute on the spot statistical analyses that kept himself, Earth, safe. Rick could look at an event and predict its outcome in 2.5 seconds and alter that event for perfection. That was what his mother and father had created in him as they became a joyous couple and switched from chaos to complementing each other. Rick only knew how to question life and analyze life. He felt something was missing and unbalanced; he felt like a slave to what protected Earth.

The Beyond Us agent could see through Astor detectives that Rick's aura was unbalanced, so the powers that be decided to send Sky. Sky had the superpower to change the weather and play with Rick's outcomes. Sky wanted to help Rick become available to the Beyond Us.

One morning, while Rick was astral-projecting around Earth with the thoughts of his mind, he found nothing unbalanced and was pleased. With calm and ease, Rick took a nap. While he was napping, Sky let it rain, and the rain flooded the whole planet.

Upon waking, Rick, during his normal rounds, could not understand why, with his perfect calculations, the planet had allowed a flood without Earth's permission while he was napping. Rick was angry and soaked in self-pity, blaming himself for napping when Earth needed protection. His aura grew gray, and he put clouds in the atmosphere. This anger turned inward was to awaken Rick to his ego and its illusion of perfection. He defended his methods repeatedly, yet the flood remained, and he remained without answers as to why the world had flooded. This frustrated Rick to no end. His anger became lightning and thunder on Earth as a result of his low-grade mood.

Sky offered Rick an olive branch. Rick, if willing to meditate, would have understood that something beautiful was from his surrendering of Earth, for no one could own Earth. Rick could not stomach that uncertainty, and he began to blame Liz and Joe for his inability to balance himself. All of Rick's astral analyses were

23

effective, so he started to question his reality. Rick felt that Earth had been somehow compromised because of his mistakes. Rick did not understand divine intervention and how a mess could disguise something life-altering for the betterment of Earth.

Sky, the Beyond Us agent, understood Rick would have to learn to allow things to be and face his fear of not being in control, for he was not in control in the first place.

He went over and over in his head his scientific analysis of the weather forecast prior to his nap, and no rain was detected, let alone a flood. Rick thought to himself, *This is impossible!* His parents, Liz and Joe, had warned him that when it was time to transmute into his full potential, he would be changed by an unpredictable experience, so Rick, for the first time, stopped in his tracks. He looked around, observing his life and all his decisions, asking himself if the Beyond Us agents were trying to send him a message. In that surrender, he took a big breath and breathed it out, relaxing his whole body and putting the ocean into place. Now Earth was 70 percent water.

Rick had no idea that breath and time of relaxation to empty his mind would create a life force. Trees, flowers, and fruits were created. Rick saw that it was great, and he praised his creation of vegetation. He looked at the ocean and saw that it was beautiful, and he praised it. Rick never could have foreseen that a flood and his surrender would create so much vegetation, liberation, and glory. Sky's mission was complete. Rick had learned to surrender and transmute Earth with his energy to create a life force. Sky foresaw that Rick would meet his soul mate due to the level of meditation and his newfound ability to self-calm. Anything was possible with surrendering to the art of allowing the source of all life force to take control.

CHAPTER 6

BENEFITS OF SURRENDERING

While observing his creation, which reflected himself, Rick could smell a pleasant scent lingering in the air. It was definitely his lily of the valley. Rick thought to himself, *Lily of the valley only grows in the garden,* so he went to see the location of the pleasant smell lingering in the air. With no luck, he found nothing. There was no trace of a lily of the valley in sight, but its fleeting smell hung in the air thickly.

He didn't know that Violet had taken the lily of the valley and bathed with it in the ocean; thus, the pleasant smell filled Earth. Violet had been intrigued by the beauty of Earth so much that she had come from Third Eye, the planet that had awakened Rick's parents into harmonious joy.

Rick, since learning to relax and enjoy the beauty of allowing life, having painted beautifully on his canvas with no effort of his own, was able to wait patiently for the source. Little did he know it was Violet. He closed his eyes and breathed in and out, relaxing his whole body. He could feel something great happening to him. He felt a wave of euphoric bubbles tingling over his whole body. This was his third-eye activation. He felt peace in that peace. He heard his Beyond Us agent, Sky, whisper to him, "Open your eyes; she is here."

Rick immediately opened his eyes as Violet rode by on her levitating motorcycle, which was ultraviolet purple. He yelled for Violet to stop, but she did not hear him, for she vibrated at a frequency of peaceful surrender Rick was not tapped in to or turned on to completely. Sky instructed Rick to softly whisper in a loving tone for Violet to stop. Rick whispered from his heart and soul, "Please join me for time in the garden. I know you like lily of the valley, and there are plenty here in the garden."

Violet halted her floating motorcycle and landed on Earth. She took her shoes off and walked on the warm ocean water from the edge of the ocean all the way to Rick.

Rick could hardly contain himself. He could see her bright purple eyes radiating from afar, her dark purple hair flowing in the air, and her evanescent silver face and purple leather bodysuit from a distance. In seconds, she was in the garden, where he was facing and overlooking the ocean. He was smitten by her beautiful, radiant, peaceful confidence from miles away. He had to breathe slowly, for she was taking his breath away faster than he could catch it the closer she was to his proximity.

She said, "Hello. You must be responsible for all this beauty upon Earth, including the flowers and delicious fruits I have indulged upon."

Rick became still and said, "No, not I alone."

Violet became intrigued. "If you are not responsible, then who is?"

Rick said, "I played a role in all there is, and my parents also played a role in all there is, as they are the sun that gives to Earth the light energy we enjoy right now. The same all there is caused me to relax and breathe, and my breath gave energy to Earth to grow. I am part of the all and all. I used to think I was somehow separate from the whole, so I stressed over my own calculations of perfection. Now I know I am perfection, and I am part of all perfection. The sound of the Beyond Us was made in that divine intelligence: om."

Violet and Rick, in that spiritual moment of knowing themselves, coupled repeatedly. They coupled until their bodies were full of kinetic energy, and they were able to occupy each other's space on every level as they moved up and down and round and round. The Beyond Us was now the place where Violet and Rick worshipped in peace and joy. That had not always been the case; both had a flashback to centuries prior, when Violet had been a temple lover. Violet had thought in those days that her body was her only worth and that she had nothing else to offer love with. Things seemed simple for Violet and Rick, but Violet and Rick had four billion years to work out the difficulties.

CHAPTER 7

◆

PAST LIVES

After years of working in the temple of love, Violet learned she was part of something bigger than herself, for she could give her customers pleasure. She could make their fantasies come true. Being a pleaser was Violet's specialty. She felt no insecurities with her body. In her various pleasure-filled escapades, Violet understood coupling. She knew that something beyond her in the moment of ecstasy was happening. Violet would watch and observe her customers while they were in a state of gratification. Some customers would shake. Some customers would moan. Most customers would rain from their members showers of pleasurable rain juices, and those sexual releases flowed through the temple day after day. Violet remembered meeting Rick centuries ago in that same temple.

The temple was created for royal people to explore their sexual desires. Rick was a king, and Violet was a temple pleasure worker, until she met the king and became a temple lover. Violet was in the temple with an aura that was gray. She felt empty after every sexual encounter, and somehow, she could feel herself fading away. A part of Violet felt depleted after giving so much pleasure to person after person with no deeper connection than lust. Deep down in Violet's being, she knew there was something deeper and more intimate about coupling she had not yet experienced, perhaps the Beyond Us.

The temple was all about outward beauty and fulfillment of the body's muscles fully contracting and releasing with no connection to the soul. Violet explained this in terms of one indulging in too much sugar and, as a result, developing rotting teeth. Love was the only way to have this much pleasure without decay. As gorgeous as Violet looked, she felt a hole inside her and needed a spiritual root canal. For her, sugar was too sweet and rotting out her inner beauty. She appeared radiant on the outside: she had red-painted lips and long, flowing dark red hair; was clothed in silk with lavender and red lace; and smelled like a soothing lavender plant. But her soul needed substance that only love could give.

When Rick came in with a turquoise aura, he saw her and chose Violet out of all the temple pleasure workers available. Violet was able to make all his fantasies come true. Rick liked to fix females' auras that were gray like Violet's. Rick's physical ego and emotional ego were now invested in the case of Violet. She had a low sense of self, if any self left. Violet, as she had been taught, started sucking, turning over, and taking Rick's male member into her warm mouth, and honey flowed from his male member all the way down her throat. As she swallowed his honey with pleasure, he looked at her right in her eyes, seeing nothing but a lifeless dark gray shell, and his eyes were bright turquoise.

Rick and Violet coupled repeatedly that evening. She felt no guilt or shame; she felt numb in the temple. She was a machine. She felt like a slave to everyone who came into that temple. Her body was used by many for their profit. Violet was a perfect assignment for Rick. He needed to be good at something, and he chose Violet to succeed at.

Rick was a nearby king in need of some stress relief. Rick's kingly duties were becoming a nightmare. Rick's wife, Mrs. Ruby, found out about Rick coming to the pleasure temple to be pleased. Rick no longer enjoyed coupling with his wife and turned her down night after night with various excuses. Queen Ruby was infuriated and planned to end her husband's coupling adventures at the temple.

Rick came home skipping, hopping, and acting as if a load of negative energy had been released after his time spent with Violet. Rick fell head over heels for Violet and made her his regular pleasure temple worker, calling her his queen of the night. Rick paid off Violet's debts owed to the pleasure temple owner.

Rick's wife, Ruby, hired her best servant to spy and find out whom Rick loved more than her. The spy reported that Violet was the one who allowed Rick the space to be himself. The spy reported that she was a master of seduction. Queen Ruby ordered her spy to have Violet's life taken away at once in a violent rage.

Violet was electromagnetically burned alive. Before Rick and Violet could have a child, for Violet was pregnant, she was obliviated. Violet had hoped to meet Rick again as a free woman and give him a child in honor of his paying all her debts. However, right after Rick paid for Violet's freedom, she was murdered.

Rick and Violet's destiny became a reality through patience, long suffering, and much wisdom. Rick investigated Violet's soul, and he confirmed all she said with no words. They met in the temple of pleasure and had their chance to become one for the first time. It took their souls four billion years to meet again. The ceremony took place in the Beyond Us as Rick and Violet gave birth to Moon. Finally, Moon, Rick and Violet's baby girl, was able to reflect the sun's joy and love for Earth. Violet admired her beautiful, glowing Moon just the way she was, including Moon's gravitational pull on the ocean. Everything on Earth was restorative. Rick and Violet's enjoyment was positively influenced by their daughter, Moon.

However, Moon inherited energetically Violet's guilt and shame from previous lives. The Beyond Us had a way of making each generation earn their cosmic existence through overcoming weakness and obstacles, even some weaknesses paid forward.

CHAPTER 8

─◆─

THE MOON

The moon was born on the planet of Crown Spiritual, and her name was Mona. Mona was taught by her forefathers to reflect the sun's light. Mona had no revelation of why she was reflecting the sun's light. She was instructed to honor her parents, Rick and Violet, by giving light to the void dark places of Earth. The moon, as Mona, gave homage for Rick's surrender and enough light for Violet's astral projections at any given time. Violet was now unhindered; since the moon was alive, she could astral-project all over the world with daylight and moonlight. She traveled at the speed of light, and those who were in the Beyond Us could see her pure dust and smell her lily-of-the-valley perfume. Mona gave balance to honor her father, but that very balance her father, Rick, no longer attached himself to. Sky's unpredictable weather of rain that flooded Earth caused chaos. Earth, Rick, surrendered, and out of chaos came photosynthesis. That photosynthesis attracted Violet.

Mona, like the sun and Earth, had a lesson to learn. Soon she would explore what that lesson was. Mona was noble. She reflected her family's legacy, and she did so gracefully with her magnificent glow, which compared to no one else's glow. On the fiftieth evening of Crown Spiritual, Mona astral-projected onto Earth as a woman. She wept loudly, saying, "I am so tired of being what everyone else wants me to be."

Mona cried so loudly a nearby shape-shifter named Darrick came running. Before Darrick could get to her, Mona walked into the ravenous, crashing waves. She was immediately launched out into the depths of the sea. Darrick shape-shifted into a merman. He walked into the water, activating his fin. Darrick, as a merman, searched for Mona with all his might.

Mona was at the bottom of the ocean, in the form of a seashell. He picked her up and took her to the ocean shore. He left her there to feel comfortable enough to come out of her shell.

Mona stayed in her shell. Darrick knew this because every day, he came by in turtle form to check on Mona. Sand was forced into her shell, and she was infected by a parasite and became hardened. Mona was now a pearl. A beautiful pearl Mona was. She woke up gasping for air. Earth went without light for three days and three nights, for Mona stayed in her shell. The moon had no idea her astral projection was so powerful. She had the ability to become any form of anything on Earth for as long as three days, but Earth went without light at night as a result. She could assume whatever form of existence she could think of before waking up as the moon again on the third day in the evening. This gift of astral projection and shape-shifting was given to the moon goddess, Mona, as a tool for obtaining knowledge.

One night, Mona fell asleep and astral-projected to Earth as a human being. Once again, she was crying loudly; her soul felt the pain of Violet's guilt and shame from past lives' mistakes. Mona's cry was so loud and intense that the same shape-shifter, Darrick, recognized the pain in her voice and came running, this time faster, as he did not want to search the entire ocean for Mona's hiding spot. She had no intention of hiding from her pain this time. When Darrick found Mona, he wept with empathy beside her. He put his arms around her and listened to her cry so much that he recognized her cry from all other cries. He listened to Mona's inner state of being so much that he taught her to listen to herself. Darrick was a great mirror for Mona.

After listening for thirteen years to an entire history of Mona's passed-down pain, hurt, guilt, and shame, Darrick felt released to help Mona complete her healing process. Darrick said, "Let me take you somewhere."

She agreed, but Darrick gave a condition: "In order for you to go with me, you must be authentic! You must overcome this victim stance." He stared intently into Mona's eyes. "I smell the 'I am stuck' mode. I smell the 'Give up' spirit, and this attitude will get us kicked out. With just one trace of the 'I am not worthy' or 'I am a victim' aroma, we could become nonexistent in the land of the Beyond Us. In the Beyond Us, the frequencies do not allow any negative stations."

Mona thought to herself, *How can I clean myself of the unworthiness?* She was infected by a poison of guilt and shame; the root of unforgiven shortcomings in her mother's past had fruition in her life. Mona had tried to heal her inherited pain by running away from her pain, crying out her pain, and even questioning her existence. However, the wisdom of the shape-shifter knew that type of infection must be cut out, and she must heal from the inside out.

This questioning penetrated Mona's aura for the first time, and she realized she could change her state of being. She took in all the sadness, giving it a name: My Mother's Pain. My Mother's Pain's energy carried with it a vacuum. This vacuum she felt trapped in for 70 percent of the time, until she was baptized by her mind's new thinking, which was 30 percent positive energy. Positive energy carried a much different, lighter vibration than past pain's energy. Mona called her sadness Violet's Pain, which reflected nothing of Mona. Her mother's pain was dark matter repelling light. Mona further understood why her aura smelled so bad: because she did not understand who she was as an individual outside her mother's pain.

Her mother had not given her validation. Everyone said her glow compared to none, yet she felt empty. Was that why she glowed? Just for her family's fulfillment? Or was there a deeper reason for Mona's glow? The reasoning for her glow Mona feared the most. The ignorance of her mother was manifested fear of the self, for knowledge of the self was the unknown.

She took a glimpse from her aura and a whiff of her pain and her heart's longing of wanting more, and with that truth, Mona shifted her suppressed energy into an authentic self-discovery. Now Mona was ready to learn why she glowed as the moon. In that moment of clarity, she stared at the reflection of herself for the first time and fell in love with her soul. She did not see her body, her skin color, her hair, or anything materialistic or tangible; she saw her soul. The moon's soul was bright like a white opal rainbow and awe-inspiring. There were no words to describe it. Her soul was crystal clear. She felt purpose—no longer purpose from her mother's guilt and shame, other people's perspectives, or other people's opinions but from her being. She felt fulfilled—om.

Mona exhaled and relaxed, and that night, the new moon was born. No matter the dark energy, no matter the illusion of dark energy or positive energy, Mona used that energy to discover her authentic self. Mona no longer judged herself as better or worse but saw herself as part of the whole, the all in all. She saw her inner beauty, and that enlightened her to fulfill her purpose and glow from the inside out. She realized she could not compare herself to anyone. The moon stood alone, but she was not alone; she was part of all there was, the Beyond Us.

There were many Beyond Us agents. Each agent knocked on the door and said, "Enough *me*. Get still. Be still. You are, in fact, the stillness that is the Beyond Us. When we speak of the Beyond Us, we are speaking of the personalization of things, ownership. We defend things, defend ourselves, defend our past, and defend our thought processes, and we create unnecessary suffering. We create a *me* from a place of 'I am not good enough,' as if we are not connected to all there is. We are not aware of the all in all. The connections of the Beyond Us are not lacking. It is all there is—om—and will ever be, the space to be. The Beyond Us!"

With her newfound authenticity, Mona attracted shape-shifter Darrick, who decided to show the moon his original state: darkness itself. Darrick was the night, which had worshipped the moon since both of their births. Darrick got so dark he made even the oldest star that much brighter. Darkness was so thick in his aura that Mona shone as a full moon. Mona fell in love with the darkness that was

Darrick. She looked into Darrick's black eyes and felt part of him as one. She looked at his black skin and understood Darrick was also translucent and had every color deep within. Mona felt every color of the rainbow in Darrick's presence, for it was full of pleasure.

Darrick, when in human form, had black skin. His hair was black, his eyes were black, his boots were black, and his bodysuit was black. Mona felt comfortable in that they were both void of color. Mona, in human form, was white. She had white skin, white hair, a white bodysuit, and white boots. The couple were both void of color but elicited colorful emotions.

Mona, in the form of the moon, fell in love with Darrick as the darkness of the night—so much so that they romanced each other to crescent moon, waxing moon, half moon, full moon, and new moon, giving each other space for their love to grow. Many could not see the darkness, but it honored the moon and night's coupling and complementing of each other's best qualities. Mona and Darrick were made for each other. The moon and darkness had respect for each other and eclipsed in full circling, for one experience of eclipse was felt forever. Mona and Darrick could feel that state of ecstasy in every eclipse when they became one and in every cycle of the moon. Mona felt free to leave her mother's past mistakes in the past, for she was the daughter of Violet, and Violet would soon learn to take responsibility for her own deeds.

CHAPTER 9

THE QUEEN

"I had Violet murdered. Why do I feel no satisfaction?" Queen Ruby asked herself. "My king, Rick, comes home now and has a gray countenance. He sits on his plush red sofa, staring out the window, gazing as if remembering great times with Violet. That slut of a whore! I thought after I had her killed, I would feel his love once again. Now all I bear are secret deaths—the whore's death and my husband's emotional death. He is walking around like an empty, soulless man. His body is alive, he is breathing, and he is maintaining his kingly duties, but like a dull knife that does not cut, I feel nothing between us but a dull ache within my heart.

"A comma in a sentence changes the meaning with no new words added, for the significance is not the words; it is the pause or the break. That is us with our deeds! One bad decision has changed our entire relationship. I just wanted my husband to love me at all costs! I wanted him to feel excited the way he felt excited to be with her. I am the queen, and I get whatever I want. If I cannot have what I want, then no one can have it. Becoming the queen was no easy task. Many women wanted Rick; I had to outshine, outdo, and outplay them. Now all my master-manipulation tactics have dulled my husband's heart toward me.

"This weight I carry is crippling me with guilt and shame. I am locked in a prison of my own secrets, and no matter how I dress up my pain, I am dull! I wear a crown of rubies. I dress in gold jewelry. I wear the finest clothing from all the world's finest fabrics, but I feel ragged! I feel empty. I feel lost. I do not know whom I can talk to! I do not know whom I can rely on. I do not see myself anymore. I look at our pictures, and I see the woman I use to be. I am no longer her anymore. How do I even start the conversation? There have been years with so much said in the thickness of the silence. I cannot keep silent any longer.

"My master manipulation has gotten dangerous for me! I do not feel his love for me any longer. I do not feel my own love, and I question all I have been taught. I question everything I once thought mattered. Look at me—I have attained all I desire, but I have nothing! I have nothing without true love."

The Beyond Us agents now could come to Queen Ruby's rescue because she was finally authentic. An agent had whispered softly in her ear all along, but now she could hear the whispers because she was open and receptive. She was no longer lying to herself. She was now listening to her inner guide.

The queen lay in the middle of the floor, weeping at the top of her lungs. With every tear she cried, she felt poisons and toxins leaving her body. She cried tears so large and so numerous that she made a puddle of tears on the floor.

The Beyond Us agent began dialoguing with her about love. "Love is not control. Love surrounds all but does not encapsulate anything. It does not own any one person, place, or thing. Love is all there is, and love has no disconnect. Love is the space it gives, the acceptance it has, and the compassion it breeds. If you knew love, felt love, and had an intimate relationship with love, you would be able to give it, Queen Ruby. We do not put you down for not knowing what love is. We understand that you were not aware of how much love is you, is through you, and is surrounding you. Love is you, Queen Ruby.

"You saw the whore in Violet and killed her, but you were projecting. You are much like a temple lover looking for love through trying to be good enough with a title or duty. Now you know her pain. Now you understand how it feels to bear things you cannot take back. Now you know your husband's pain. It is all pain. Your pain has blinded you for years, but now your pain has pushed you to see yourself. Beyond your pain, shame, guilt, and mistakes is a little girl who never felt loved. Becoming the queen, wearing your expensive clothing, eating the finest of foods, drinking the best wines—all you did was for the little girl's need for acceptance and validation. Being a little girl in a grown-up body with money and power is dangerous. You are now growing up, and this is the consequence of the not-good-enough false reality you were accustomed to. You have lost the love of your life, King Rick, by trying to own him. Now the temple lover is dead, but so is your love with Rick. You must confess your faults, Ruby, to King Rick and, no matter how harsh the consequences, move forward, or you risk being stuck in madness!"

Queen Ruby stopped crying and paced the floors, contemplating how she would tell him the truth—the whole truth. Queen Ruby's strong desire to be free was more important than living a lie. Her desire to be authentic was stronger than her desire to look the part or keep the role of queen. The queen had her maids pack up all her belongings and prepare them in case the king decided to take off her head or banish her from the castle.

Late one evening, the queen had the king's favorite meal prepared with finest dinette, and after he was nice and stuffed, the queen had a forgiveness dance performed by the talented servants to soften Rick's heart in preparation for her confession. She felt the words bubbling up from her heart, and she knew it was time to bare her unspeakable deeds. She felt like a glass filled to overflowing, so she began pouring her words into Rick's ready-to-hear ears. She explained how, from the beginning, she had plotted to be queen, removing all obstacles from the first day she met King Rick. She told him she'd dressed, flirted, and planned to seduce him, and this time, it had gone too far. Out of her clenched throat, she mumbled, "I killed her. Not with my hands but by my command. I had Violet murdered."

Immediately, the king thought to himself, *Ruby discovered my indiscretions.* He said, "But how did you know, Ruby?"

The queen said, "I felt your heart turn towards Violet in a way that your heart never turned towards me. Rick, I witnessed right before my eyes your skin soft and glowing with a golden light from inside out, a light only true lovers could glow! I had you followed, and I had her killed. I was jealous. I thought to myself, *How come all my manipulations to be queen succeed, and Violet, the temple whore, gets to be queen of his heart?* I wanted that. I wanted you to love me as you loved Violet. Violet did not have her freedom. Violet did not have expensive clothing, and Violet you loved. Rick, I tried to win you over, but you did not even give me a chance; you just fell for Violet. So I made an irreversible choice."

The king cried, as he knew he'd killed Queen's Ruby's heart and was guilty of getting his temple lover, Violet, killed as well. The king thought, *How could I have been such a fool to think Ruby did not notice my infidelities?* He decided to forgive the queen and gave Ruby a decree of uncircling. The uncircling was given so Ruby could find true love, for between Ruby and Rick, there was no true love, until that release. Uncircling lifted the weight of falsehood from their hearts, and there was an instant freedom to start over and make a fresh start. For the first time, King Rick could rest, and Queen Ruby had a sense of closure. In that love, a miracle soon would take place.

CHAPTER 10

THE QUEEN'S TRANSFORMATION

Ruby took some time to reflect on her current state. She was no longer a queen. She did not know who she was; she was a house with bare walls, no furniture, and nothing at all, just an empty house. She sat in the forest, under a pine tree beside a lake. She could see and smell the lavender plants growing within reach. Ruby could smell the relaxation of the forest and the richness it offered after the rain. She could hear the water streaming nearby. For the first time in Ruby's life, she felt at peace.

Ruby thought about where this peace was coming from. Ruby no longer needed a man, and she no longer required the title of a queen to feel secure. She had conquered a king and been a queen with her manipulative ways. She had gotten away with having her king's mistress, Violet, killed. Firsthand, Ruby had seen how cruel jealousy could be. She had risked being killed by the king to rid herself of deceit, lies, and cruelty. Ruby repented with a sincere heart. She was forced to leave her familiarity into the unknown. She had to start all over again and build a home from scratch and a garden for survival.

Day by day, Ruby became anew. She painted her walls lilac. She swept her floors, swept down the cobwebs, washed the walls, and mopped the floors with lavender-oil soap. She made the soap with her bare hands. She created a table with nearby wood. She fashioned curtains and a tablecloth for the table. She worked vigorously on building every integral part of her home. Every detail of her home was from her heart.

All the work attracted her soul mate, Ruby's true lover. Finally, she had a lover who loved her for her. Ruby did nothing but present her authentic self. She called herself Ola. He was Mo, a nearby knight of King Rick, whom Ruby was divorced from. She no longer wore a crown from Rick's kingdom, but for the first time, Ruby, as Ola, felt as if she were wearing a crown of many jewels glowing from within. She felt her heart was now as light as a feather, and with that love, she learned to time-travel.

The first time she time-traveled, she was watching herself plot against the king's mistress, the temple lover Violet. Ruby did not understand her powers of time-travel fully. She could alter her decisions by going back in time, but she risked permanent changes that could alter her fate. Ruby, full of wisdom, asked herself a question: How far was Queen Ruby, now divinely embraced as Ola, willing to travel back in time to clear her conscience of murder and to clear the bloody hands of the man she had commanded to kill Violet? She contemplated the risk, and she could not see that far, but she concluded that the risk to try to right her wrongs was worth it. Ruby, with wisdom and now renamed Ola, understood that to free herself from negative choices, she had to time-travel back.

Ola went back in time but realized if she changed anything, she might make another mistake. She figured out a way to talk to herself as a little girl through her mind's vivid imagination. She told herself a story about a jealous queen and how her jealousy led her to plot another's death and lose everything in the end. As a result, the little girl decided to be kind, loyal, grateful for what was given to her, and not envious or jealous of what someone else had that was seemingly more appealing.

In that breath of right decision-making on Ola's part, the king woke up and felt led to visit the grave site where his temple lover was buried. Lo and behold, the temple lover was not dead. She had not been electromagnetically burned to death.

The king investigated where his lover was, and after he searched and searched, he discovered that his faithful servant who had been ordered to murder the temple lover had been too scared to carry out Queen Ruby's order. The servant instead had placed a burned corpse in the temple of love as Violet. The temple lover's workers had conspired with Violet to deceive the queen and king with a staged death. Violet had been sent away to the underground world instead of being killed.

The king had her retrieved at once and brought back to the kingdom where he ruled and reigned. He cleaned Violet up and apologized to her for the trouble of the whole matter. He had a child with Violet named Mona, and they lived in circling bliss. Not only did King Rick and his lover, Violet, find bliss, but Queen Ruby found her bliss as Ola met Mo as well.

CHAPTER 11

MO AND OLA'S BLISS

Ola was smart, and she was courageous, for it took courage to be honest in the face of possible death. Ola revealed her grievous plot to murder Violet, confessing when she let go of her Queen Ruby facade. Violet was alive, but it turned out there were two deaths: the death of King Rick's ego and the death of Queen Ruby's ego. What lived on was all there really was: divine intelligence.

When Ola least expected it, a visitor arrived. Mo, a passing knight, was intrigued by her beautiful garden. The aroma of the garden washed his senses in peaceful bliss. Mo decided to ride his black horse to drink from Ola's water fountain in the middle of the lavender haven. Mo was rough; he had scars on his skin from battles lost and scars on his heart from lost love. He was tall and muscular, and he was compassionate. Mo mirrored his horse, as he was fashioned in all-black clothing, with silver trim and silver armor. His sword had a black handle and silver blade. Mo's hair was orange with red accents, his eyes were blue with a green tint, and his skin was olive. Mo had been wandering around after a battle, lost, looking for some comfort and a tender touch to console his defeated spirit. Without knowledge, he stumbled upon Ola's haven created of nearby lavender and the best fruits, nuts, and honey.

It was love at first sight. Ola had worked hard to build her life all over again; she had confidence in her walk; and in her hip's was passion for life, demonstrated in her sway. When Mo witnessed her strength as she cultivated the garden, he fell in love with her. Ola and Mo talked about their childhoods, their past relationships, and rebuilding their lives. Mo did not talk a lot, but he was a good listener; Ola felt heard and validated for the first time in her life. Mo was not silent when he listened to Ola; often, he said no words when Ola spoke, but she could hear his compassion. Mo's compassion was so loud that Ola felt empathy vibrating through her essence, and in that thickness, her soul connected to Mo, and they experienced enlightenment.

Ola conversed with Mo about how he had become a great listener. Mo took a deep breath and explained to Ola that he once had been in a prison of pain where no one heard his heart's desire to understand why his parents were dead. Ola, having learned to listen from Mo, joined in the conversation by never saying a word but listening with love.

Mo said, "It all started when I was a boy. My mother and father both died when I was about eleven years old. I remember my mother and father talking and laughing often. My mother was a creative person. She painted beautiful art, and people would come from afar to buy her beautiful art collections. My father was a knight like myself. He would ride his horse, a black stallion like mine, and defend the king. I remember my mother cooking, cleaning, and taking care of my father and me with joy. My mother's smile could bring the promise of hope to anyone's gloomy day.

"I found my father and mother in their bed, lifeless, on a cold winter day. I remember it as if it were yesterday. I dug graves for my parents side by side in our family's backyard, near my parents' favorite apricot tree. During the summer, my mother would lie underneath the apricot tree after picking so many apricots that she could not carry the basket. My father would come kiss her under that tree and carry the apricots into the house. I always knew she pretended the basket was too heavy so my father could come get the basket and kiss her.

"I cried in that very spot where her body lay beneath the earth under the apricot tree. My tears then turned to a trumpet of pain as I rumbled out a cry from my lungs. No one heard the cry for help, and no one came to my rescue, but what showed up was the part of me that my parents had cultivated in love. I was an only child, I had never met any of my parents' family, and I felt abandoned. I was just an eleven-year-old boy. Thanks to my parents, I could eat of the land and survive, for everything I needed was right on the land. My parents, since the day I was born, had taught me how to take care of myself. By the time I was eleven years old, I could survive but not thrive. I longed for love, affection, and to be heard. I wanted answers.

"With my intentions clear, at twelve years old, I rode my horse—a black one just like my father's—to the king's castle, and I pledged allegiance to the king and took on the training to become a knight. I never knew why my parents died. I just found them dead in their bed. I never revealed I was a son of a knight. I learned to ask questions and listen to find out why my parents died. My parents seemed healthy and seemed to be favored by the king and queen, so I was on a quest to discover the reason for their deaths. That is why I am a knight: I wanted to defend my family's honor and find out why my parents were taken away from me.

"I searched for the answers day after day. As I searched, I grew stronger and stronger, working out daily my mind and my body for the day I could avenge my mother and father. I became obsessed with how to discern a person's lie from the truth. My soul needed rest, but I refused to rest until I discovered the truth. I never did discover this truth. It seemed no one knew the reason my parents died. No one knew I was the knight's son. I had my own features, which differed from my mother's and father's features."

Ola offered to help Mo discover what had happened to his parents. She took him by the hands, and to her surprise, she did not see a happy mother in her mind or a father. Ola cried and grabbed Mo, offering to take him to his mother at once, for she was still alive.

Mo said, "No, Ola, there must be a mistake in your reading, for my mother and father are dead."

Ola was sure of what she had discovered and had no doubt, for her love had been tested many times. She had touched his hands, picking up his DNA, and time-traveled to Mo's biological parents' time together. Mo was shocked but willing to go with this newfound evidence. Ola gathered their belongings and time-traveled, taking Mo to where she saw his mother. His mother was on planet V.

When Mo and Ola arrived on planet V, they heard wishful sounds humming and buzzing to their bones of women pledging never to hurt one another and to look after one another. The leader of the group was Ivy. Mo and Ola walked through an all-white ceremony of women singing and dancing in celebrating feminine energy.

Mo looked at Ivy and felt a different connection, one he never had felt before: a connection to his mother who'd reared him. Mo and Ivy finally reconnected. Ivy explained to Mo that he was the son of Joe—a secret child. Ivy told Mo how she had met Joe. Ultimately, she had discovered he was married and left him but with his child inside her. Ivy talked about wanting to rear Mo but knowing of a couple who always had wanted a child but could not have any, for they did not want to physically have any children.

"I gave you to them, and on your twelfth birthday, they were to give you back to me. The plan was that I would tell you who your father was and how to meet your father. Would you like to meet your father, Mo?"

Mo replied, "Yes, Mother," while consoling her.

Ivy said, "Look up! Your father is the sun."

Mo said in shock, "The sun?"

Ivy explained, "Your father is a superbeing. He became the sun, and his creation with his wife became your world. This earth is your brother. Son, you have super DNA. Every fiber of your being can connect with your family. This universe is your family, and you are this universe's family; there is no separation to who you are."

Mo recalled crying when the only parents he had known died and not understanding why his family did not answer his call. Now he understood that his process of coming into his own identity had required him to experience loss, even the loss of his dear parents who'd reared him.

With a deep breath, Mo closed his eyes and was united with his father, Joe; stepmother, Liz; and brother, Rick, in spirit. Mo's father apologized to him for not being there for him and explained that he wanted to be there now. Mo's stepmother and brother apologized too. Forgiveness was extended, and the contract for Mo to avenge his parents' deaths was released. Mo finally felt his heart at peace. Now, with Mo's surfaced superpowers, he could commune with his parents and brother anytime for love, guidance, and connection.

Mo looked at Ivy and Ola with gratitude and ease, saying it was all worth it. He told them he'd made sure he lost battles if he could not guarantee 100 percent that he could win the battle to live long enough to discover why his parents had died. Mo now understood that every battle he'd lost and his feelings of defeat had been for this day of winning the war he'd decided to take on at twelve years old. Mo now understood he never had been abandoned; he had been guided the whole time to the reality that he was connected to all there was and the Beyond Us.

After they returned to Earth from planet V, daily dialogues between Ola and Mo continued, and they felt inseparable from each other. Mo decided to ask Ola for her hand in circling in the garden where they first had met. Mo felt so much gratitude for Ola being in his life; she was instrumental in his healing and in his finding forgiveness.

Mo prepared a lunch on top of a dark purple blanket on a meadow near a brook. He gathered the best fruits, nuts, and honey from the garden to indulge and created a delectable dish with the fruits and honey. He walked to the house and asked Ola to come outside. Ola agreed and made her way out the door.

Mo took Ola by the hand and led her to the romantic spot prepared with care. He laid her down and massaged her body with lavender oil. He whispered in her ear, "You are enough! You are more than enough, in fact. I want to pledge my gratitude for you."

He poured two glasses of fine wine homemade with lavender and grapes he had fermented some years ago for a special occasion such as this. They enjoyed the fine wine and dining as they laughed together. Ola laughed so hard she lay on her stomach, kicking her legs in overwhelming joy. Once Mo felt her body relax, he began kissing her neck softly while sitting on her back with his legs open and his weight on his knees. He deeply massaged Ola's entire body from her feet all the way up to her head. He laid her arms out and massaged them and clutched the ring he had bought to propose to her. He placed the ring on his pinkie finger as he massaged Ola's body continuously.

Mo intended the proposal to be a sign of his love. He lay next to her, grabbed her hand, and placed the ring on her finger. It fit with ease.

Ola jumped up, looking at the ring, and asked Mo what the ring was for. Mo told Ola the ring was a circle representing his never-ending love for her. Ola cried tears of joy and leaped with excitement.

Mo had heard Ola's heart and knew she wanted to be loved, desired, and accepted. She thought, *Could it be? Mo, a knight, has ridden into my life on a black horse and taken the time to learn who I am—the good, the not so good, and everything about me—yet still loves me and is choosing me. Wow.*

For the first time, Ola said no words. She felt a euphoric feeling as they embraced each other, and for the first time, they came full circle. Mo took all Ola's clothing off and massaged her entrance with his key made perfectly for unlocking her to all sorts of pleasure. Ola never had known she could cry tears of joy from circling. She never had known she could rain from her body beautiful showers of pleasure. Mo and Ola experienced nirvana.

Mo and Ola meditated together daily in the garden and lived in service to couples and individuals passing through who needed healing. They represented the space among the stars that allowed the stars to shine in its compassion. It took much courage for Mo and Ola to understand each other's heart, and it was the purest intention of each to provide the other with never-ending love. Mo and Ola had no children and lived in marital bliss. They provided for all who came from afar a comfortable place to rest and offered the best of the land's lavender-and-grape wine, fruits, nuts, and honey. Often, when other couples came by the beautiful lavender estate, Mo and Ola would listen with compassion, and the couples would leave having learned the ability to listen to each other.

As the years went by, Ola and Mo gained a reputation for their lavender field of love for couples in need of a tune-up. The Beyond Us had a way of helping those they helped to become change agents. Mo and Ola were truly change agents as they helped people learn to listen to one another with compassion and forgive one another for healing until they let go of their physical bodies. Mo and Ola lived together in service to others and themselves until old age. Ola died at one hundred years old, and Mo died the next day at one hundred years old as well. They were best friends.

EPILOGUE

Love is looking for an opportunity to love, and it will cultivate love continuously. No matter where a person is on the journey to the Beyond Us, love is willing to endure and conquer. This love is seen in the universe. We are the universe; we are the space in between everything. We are the light and the absence that allows the light to be seen. Love has the power to transform ordinary people into superbeings. We all have superpowers, and with courage, we can unlock the door to our highest potential. It is time. If you are reading this book, it is your time to write the next chapter of your life, and you know what that requires. It requires the Beyond Us.

Printed in the United States
by Baker & Taylor Publisher Services

Printed in the United States
by Baker & Taylor Publisher Services